Creator of All,

Thank you for everyday
miracles:

for spider webs shining
with rainbows,

for golden honey on warm biscuits,

and for cricket symphonies.

And thank you for the greatest miracle of all:
the birth, life, death, and resurrection
of your Son, Jesus.

Help us to know your miracles in our lives

and to share our gifts
with everyone we meet.

Amen.

Spider's Gift

A Christmas Story

Written by Geraldine Ann Marshall
Illustrated by Rebecca Sorge

Pauline
BOOKS & MEDIA
Boston

Library of Congress Cataloging-in-Publication Data

Names: Marshall, Geraldine Ann, author. | Sorge, Rebecca, illustrator.
Title: Spider's gift : a Christmas story / written by Geraldine Ann Marshall
    ; illustrated by Rebecca Sorge.
Description: Boston : Pauline Books & Media, [2015] | Summary: Present at
the
    birth of Jesus, Cricket sings a lullaby, Honeybee presents honey, and
    Spider wonders what she can give.
Identifiers: LCCN 2015034936 (print) | LCCN 2016010126 (ebook) | ISBN
    9780819890580 (pbk.) | ISBN 0819890588 (pbk.) | ISBN 9780819890597
(epub)
    | ISBN 9780819890603 (mobi) | ISBN 9780819890610 (pdf)
Subjects: LCSH: Jesus Christ--Nativity--Juvenile fiction. | CYAC: Jesus
    Christ--Nativity--Fiction. | Christmas--Fiction. | Spiders--Fiction. |
    Gifts--Fiction.
Classification: LCC PZ7.1.M3728 Sp 2015 (print) | LCC PZ7.1.M3728 (ebook) |
    DDC [E]--dc23
LC record available at http://lccn.loc.gov/2015034936

Illustrated by Rebecca Sorge

Design by Mary Joseph Peterson, FSP

Published by Pauline Books & Media, 50 Saint Paul's Avenue, Boston, MA
02130–3491

Printed in Korea.

SGCS SIPSKOGUNKYO4-12053 9058-8

www.pauline.org

Pauline Books & Media is the publishing house of the Daughters of St. Paul,
an international congregation of women religious serving the Church with
the communications media.

1 2 3 4 5 6 7 8 9   20 19 18 17 16

For my daughters,
Audrey and Rachel,
for whom I wrote the Christmas stories.

For our family dogs
who've all given us their gifts of love:
Scamper, Frank Lloyd, Newton,
Wilbur, Stuart Little, Emmett;
and two cats,
Charlotte and Sac a dos.

In an animal stable in the town of Bethlehem,
were a field cricket, an independent honeybee,
and an ordinary brown spider.

"Today, I want to make music," Cricket said.

"I want to dance," Honeybee said.

"Each one of my eight legs is twitching with joy," Spider said.

"Something special is going to happen!" the three friends shouted.

That night a gentle man helped a young woman with soft, dark hair into the stable. The man put clean hay in a corner for the tired woman. The woman's stomach was large and round.

"She's going to have a baby," Cricket whispered.

"Oh, Joseph," the woman said, "is this where we'll be staying?"

"All the inns are full. There is nowhere else we can go, Mary," said Joseph. He helped Mary sit on the summer-smelling hay.

"This is such a rough place to bring a baby into the world," Mary said. "But I know God will keep us safe."

Later that night, the animals awoke when a baby
began to cry. Then they heard heavenly singing, and
the stable shone with bright starlight.

Soon shepherds and their sheep entered the stable.
"We came to see if what the angel said was true,"
the eldest shepherd told Mary and Joseph. "The angel
said the Savior was born tonight."

Mary smiled, "Come and meet baby Jesus."

The shepherds knelt around the baby. "Jesus is God's best gift," a shepherd told Mary and Joseph. "Angels came to our fields. They told us of this good news for the whole world."

The shepherds gave Mary gifts for the baby. One
shepherd gave Jesus a snuggly wool blanket. The
youngest shepherd handed Mary a clay pot. When
he took the lid off, everyone in the stable could smell
sweet honey.

"Oh," said Honeybee, dancing, "that's honey my sisters and I made. Honey is *my* gift to baby Jesus."

"I'll give Jesus a gift too," announced Cricket. "I'll play him a lullaby." Cricket rubbed his wings together and made music.

Spider looked down from her web at the sleeping baby. She knew she couldn't make music like Cricket. She knew she couldn't make honey like Honeybee.

"I'm just an ordinary brown spider. I have nothing to give."

Twelve days later, three wise men came to worship baby Jesus. Each one carried a gift.

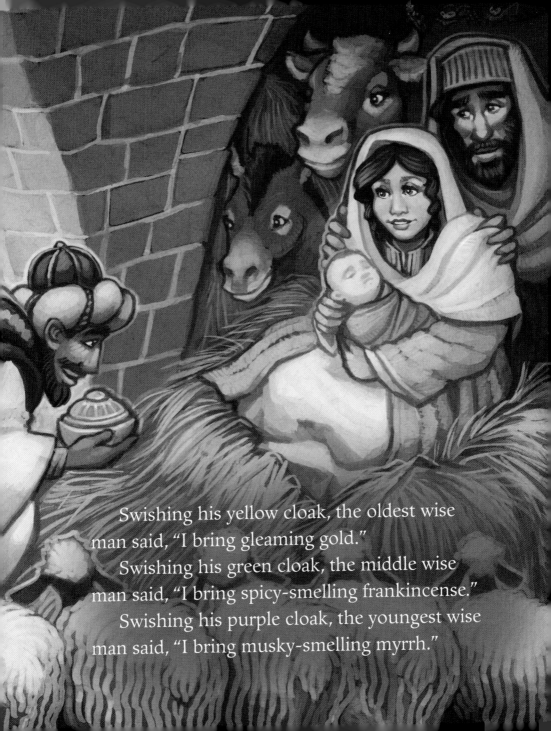

Swishing his yellow cloak, the oldest wise man said, "I bring gleaming gold."

Swishing his green cloak, the middle wise man said, "I bring spicy-smelling frankincense."

Swishing his purple cloak, the youngest wise man said, "I bring musky-smelling myrrh."

"Their gifts are almost as fine as my honey," buzzed Honeybee.

"Their gifts are almost as beautiful as my lullaby," chirped Cricket.

Spider lay on her web. "I don't have any gift for baby Jesus." And she cried herself to sleep.

Early the next morning, the three friends heard the wise men whispering to each other. "I had a dream," said the youngest.

"I had a dream, too," said the middle one.

"So did I," said the oldest, who was also the wisest. "I dreamed that King Herod is very jealous of Jesus and wants to kill him. We must leave at once and not tell Herod where to find the child."

"Will that be enough to keep baby Jesus safe from Herod?" asked the wise man in purple.

"Perhaps Herod's soldiers are already searching for Jesus," said the wise man in green.

"Those who love the child must find a way to keep him safe," said the wisest of the wise men. "They must look into their hearts for their best gifts to give." Then he looked up and winked at Spider. "God can make miracles when gifts are given with love."

Spider told her friends, "I want to keep Jesus safe. But I'm just an ordinary brown spider. I don't have any gift to give him."

"Just yesterday," said Cricket, "Jesus smiled and reached toward your web."

"Yes," agreed Honeybee. "The light made your web into a rainbow of spider silk."

"So my gift is my web?" asked Spider.

"Of course," Cricket and Honeybee said together.

"Baby Jesus gurgled and cooed at your web," Cricket chirped.

"Your web is like a small sun in this dark stable," Honeybee buzzed.

"But, can my ordinary web keep Jesus safe?"
Spider wondered. "If a web were large enough,
could it hide a whole family?"

"Maybe," said Honeybee.

Then Cricket lifted one front leg. He reminded his friends, "We crickets hear with our legs. I can hear feet marching toward our stable. It must be Herod's soldiers! They're not too close, but they are coming our way."

Oh no, thought Spider, *what can I do?* Then Spider remembered what the wisest man had said—*God can make miracles when gifts are given with love.*

"I can give my web with love!" exclaimed Spider to Cricket and Honeybee. "God can make a miracle with my web."

Spider hurried to the stable entrance and began to spin a web. She spun all day and night. She spun her finest and biggest web.

The next morning everyone in the stable heard the soldiers' stomping feet.

Through a crack in the wall, Spider saw soldiers with swords heading straight toward the stable. Mary and Joseph held their breaths and prayed that God would keep them safe.

Spider gasped. *Will my web be enough to protect Mary, Joseph, and baby Jesus? God, please use my web to keep them safe.*

Just then, sunlight bounced off her web.

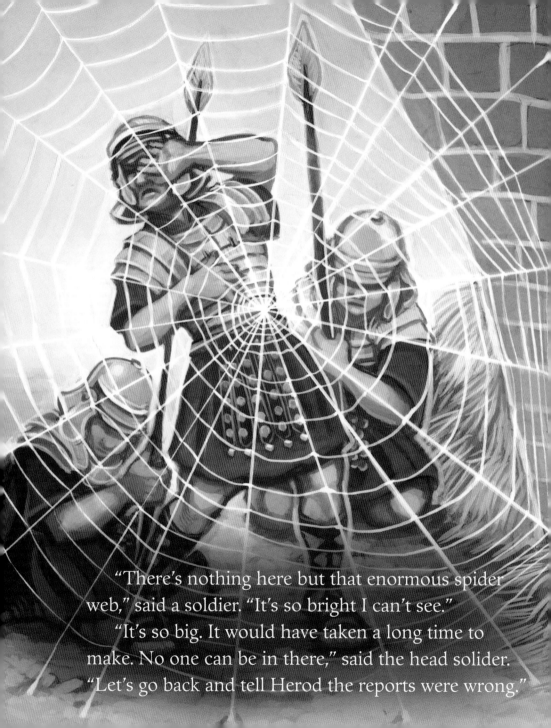

"There's nothing here but that enormous spider web," said a soldier. "It's so bright I can't see."

"It's so big. It would have taken a long time to make. No one can be in there," said the head solider.

"Let's go back and tell Herod the reports were wrong."

On the other side of the web, safe inside the stable, baby Jesus reached for Spider and smiled.

"Your web is as beautiful as a lullaby," chirped Cricket.

"Your web is as wonderful as honey," buzzed Honeybee.

And Spider knew God had used the gift of her ordinary web to keep Jesus safe.

Geraldine Ann Marshall writes books for both children and adults. She has a bachelor's degree in zoology from the University of Kentucky. She is the mother of two grown daughters. Geraldine lives in a house in the woods near Paducah, Kentucky. She shares her home with lots of wildlife, including honeybees, crickets, and even a few friendly spiders.

Geraldine

Rebecca

Rebecca Sorge loves telling stories and drawing pictures, so becoming an illustrator made perfect sense. Rebecca currently lives and works in Utah, where she enjoys creating art for children's books, magazines, posters, cards, and anything else people will let her draw on.

Tales and Legends from

Pauline kids

The 3 Trees
Adapted by Gabriel Ringlet
Illustrated by Daniella Oh

The Little Lost Lamb
Written and Illustrated
by Geri Borger Haines

the QUEEN & the CROSS
The Story of Saint Helen
Written by
Cornelia Mary Bilinsky
Illustrated by
Rebecca Stuhff

SANTA'S Secret Story
Written by
Cornelia Mary Bilinsky
Illustrated by
Candace Camling

The Saint Who Fought the Dragon
The Story of Saint George
Written by
Cornelia Mary Bilinsky
Illustrated by
Thereza Rowe

Spider's Gift
A Christmas Story
Written by
Geraldine Ann Marshall
Illustrated by
Rebecca Sorge